Playing with Plays™
Presents
Jane Austen's

Sense & Sensibility
FOR KIDS
(The melodramatic version!)

For 6-15 actors, or kids of all ages who want to have fun!
Creatively modified by Amanda Thayer & Brendan P. Kelso
Cover illustrations by Adam Watson
and Ron Leishman

**3 Melodramatic Modifications
for 3 different group sizes:**

6-9 actors

9-12 actors

11-15 actors

Table Of Contents

Foreword .... Pg 4

School, Afterschool, and Summer classes .... Pg 6

Performance Rights .... Pg 6

6-9 Actors .... Pg 8

9-12 Actors .... Pg 30

11-15 Actors .... Pg 56

Special Thanks .... Pg 82

Sneak Peeks at other Playing With Plays .... Pg 83

About the Authors .... Pg 102

To Cherice, the one with sense in our family

-BPK

To my kids for thinking I'm funny
-ART

Foreword

When I was in high school there was something about Shakespeare that appealed to me. Not that I understood it mind you, but there were clear scenes and images that always stood out in my mind. Romeo & Juliet, "Romeo, Romeo; wherefore art thou Romeo?"; Julius Caesar, "Et tu Brute"; Macbeth, "Double, Double, toil and trouble"; Hamlet, "to be or not to be"; A Midsummer Night's Dream, all I remember about this was a wickedly cool fairy and something about a guy turning into a donkey that I thought was pretty funny. It was not until I started analyzing Shakespeare's plays as an actor that I realized one very important thing, I still didn't understand them. Seriously though, it's tough enough for adults, let alone kids. Then it hit me, why don't I make a version that kids could perform, but make it easy for them to understand with a splash of Shakespeare lingo mixed in? And voila! A melodramatic masterpiece was created! They are intended to be melodramatically fun!

THE PLAYS: There are 3 plays within this book, for three different group sizes. The reason: to allow educators or parents to get the story across to their children regardless of the size of their group. As you read through the plays, there are several lines that are highlighted. These are actual lines from the original book. I am a little more particular about the kids saying these lines verbatim. But the rest, well... have fun!

The entire purpose of this book is to instill the love of a classic story, as well as drama, into the kids.

And when you have children who have a passion for something, they will start to teach themselves, with or without school.

These plays are intended for pure fun. Please DO NOT have the kids learn these lines verbatim, that would be a complete waste of creativity. But do have them basically know their lines and improvise wherever they want as long as it pertains to telling the story. Because that is the goal of an actor: to tell the story. In A Midsummer Night's Dream, I once had a student playing Quince question me about one of her lines, "but in the actual story, didn't the Mechanicals state that 'they would hang us'?" I thought for a second and realized that she had read the story with her mom, and she was right. So I let her add the line she wanted and it added that much more fun, it made the play theirs. I have had kids throw water on the audience, run around the audience, sit in the audience, lose their pumpkin pants (size 30 around a size 15 doesn't work very well, but makes for some great humor!) and most importantly, die all over the stage. The kids love it.

One last note: if you want some educational resources, loved our plays, want to tell the world how much your kids loved performing Shakespeare, want to insult someone with our Shakespeare Insult Generator, or are just a fan of Shakespeare, then hop on our website and have fun:

PlayingWithPlays.com

With these notes, I'll see you on the stage, have fun, and break a leg!

LICENSES AND ROYALTIES

All performances and other productions require the issuance of a license. Here are the basic guidelines:

1) Please contact us! We always LOVE to hear about a school or group performing our books! We would also love to share photos and brag about your program as well! (with your permission, of course)

2) We require that you purchase a copy of the play for the director/teacher and each kid in the show.

3) If you are a group and DO NOT charge your kids to be in the production, contact us about our educational rates to get a copy in each kid's hands inexpensively. (we will make this work for you!)

4) If you are a group and DO charge your kids to be in the production, (i.e. afterschool program, summer camp), contact us for bulk (10 books or more) or educator's discounts.

5) If you are a group and DO NOT charge the audience to see the plays, please see our website FAQs (www.PlayingWithPlays.com) to see if you are eligible to waive the performance license(s) (most performances are eligible).

6) If you are a group and DO charge the audience to see the performance, please see our website FAQs for performance licensing fees (this includes performances for donations and competitions).

Any other questions or comments, please see our website or email us at:
contact@PlayingWithPlays.com

The 15-Minute or so
Sense & Sensibility
for Kids

by Jane Austen
Creatively modified by
Amanda Thayer & Brendan P. Kelso
6-9 Actors
CAST OF CHARACTERS:

ELINOR: older Dashwood sister; needs to be in control; the one with sense

MARIANNE: younger Dashwood sister; loves emotion and attention; the one with sensibility

MRS. DASHWOOD: Dashwood mother; kind of kooky.

[1]**DAD:** dead dad

[2]**EDWARD:** awkward friend of the Dashwood sisters; secretly in love with Elinor

WILLOUGHBY: loves Marianne but must marry someone else because he is poor

[1]**COLONEL:** friend of Sir John; also in love with Marianne

[2]**SIR JOHN:** cousin of Mrs. Dashwood; very excited about everything all the time

[1]**SERVANT:** butler at various estates

The same actors can play the following parts:
[1]DAD, SERVANT, and COLONEL
[2]EDWARD and SIR JOHN

ACT 1 SCENE 1

(enter MRS. DASHWOOD)

MRS. DASHWOOD: Girls, come in here!

(enter ELINOR and MARIANNE)

MRS. DASHWOOD: Where's your sister?

MARIANNE: She got cut from the play.

MRS. DASHWOOD: What?!

ELINOR: She missed a bunch of rehearsals, small part, director let her go. But more importantly, mother, are you okay?

MRS. DASHWOOD: Me? I'm fine. Buuuut... your father's dead.

MARIANNE: What?! Nooooo! Dad!!!

DAD: *(offstage)* Sorry girls!

ELINOR: Poor Dad! Mom, can I get you anything? Lavender drops? Warm socks? Some chocolate cake?

MRS. DASHWOOD: You are always trying to comfort everyone, Elinor.

ELINOR: It's what I do.

MRS. DASHWOOD: Anyway, now we're super poor. Your brother and nephew inherited everything.

MARIANNE: What?! Nooooo! Dad!!!

DAD: *(offstage)* Again, sorry girls!

MARIANNE: Great. Another loss for women.

ELINOR: NO ONE PANIC! *(She pulls out a binder)*

MARIANNE: I'm not panicked. What have wealth or grandeur to do with happiness?

ELINOR: *(flipping through binder)* Everything? I have a plan for this exact situation. *(stops and points to a page)* Here we go! We all live together until men marry us and save us from poverty!

MARIANNE: Oh joy. I can't wait to be saved by a man.

MRS. DASHWOOD: *(to audience)* If you haven't figured it out yet, *(points at ELINOR)* the one with sense, *(to MARIANNE)* and sensibility.

(SERVANT enters)

SERVANT: Mr. Edward Ferrars is here to call on Miss Dashwood. *(exits)*

MARIANNE & MRS. DASHWOOD: Oooooooooh!

(enter EDWARD FERRARS)

EDWARD: Oh, hey, Elinor. Want to go for a walk or whatever? I'm not good with words. That's why I'm handsome.

ELINOR: Okay!

(exit ELINOR and EDWARD)

MARIANNE & MRS. DASHWOOD: Oooooooooh!

MRS. DASHWOOD: In a few months, my dear Marianne, Elinor will marry Edward and save us all. At least *she* will be happy.

MARIANNE: Meh. Edward is very amiable... But he is NOT handsome. And he has no real taste in art.

MRS. DASHWOOD: What does handsome have to do with love?

MARIANNE: Please mother, you're embarrassing yourself. *(motions to audience)*

MRS. DASHWOOD: He always admires Elinor's drawings very much.

MARIANNE: He admires the drawings because he likes her, not as a connoisseur. I'll never find someone to love. I require so much!

MRS. DASHWOOD: You do, Marianne. But, you aren't even seventeen. It is yet too early in life to despair of such a happiness. You can start despairing when you are twenty-one. That's when you will be an old maid.

MARIANNE: Gee, thanks, Mom.

(MARIANNE rolls her eyes; enter EDWARD and ELINOR, returning from their walk)

(enter SERVANT holding a letter on a tray)

SERVANT: A letter for Mrs. Dashwood.

MRS. DASHWOOD: *(perusing letter)* Oh! It is a letter from my cousin! He is giving us a cottage to live in now that our house has been stolen from us. We are moving to Devonshire!

EDWARD: Devonshire! Are you, indeed, going there? So far from hence!

MRS. DASHWOOD: It is but a cottage... but I hope to see many of my friends in it. *(looking at Edward)*

ELINOR: *(to audience)* I must now hide my sadness about leaving the person I am in love with. Hmmm, I know! *(to MRS. DASHWOOD)* We better get packing!

(ALL exit)

<h1 style="text-align:center">ACT 1 SCENE 2</h1>

(enter SIR JOHN; opposite ELINOR, MARIANNE, MRS. DASHWOOD)

SIR JOHN: Hello!! Welcome! I am Sir John, and I am excited about everything, all the time! *(randomly points around)* Here is the cottage. Here are the gardens. That big place over there is my house. Now you have seen everything! Isn't it wonderful??

MRS. DASHWOOD: Thank you for having us, Sir John.

SIR JOHN: Buckle up! You ladies are about to be totally social. I am forever forming parties to eat cold ham and chicken out of doors, and in winter I host loads of private balls.

MRS. DASHWOOD: You hear that, girls? So social!

SIR JOHN: However, you will only see one gentleman here besides myself. He is a particular friend who is staying at the park.

MARIANNE: At the park? Is he homeless? A poet? An artist? Does he appreciate nature? Why does he live in a park?

ELINOR: *(coughs)* We look forward to meeting your friend.

SIR JOHN: Great! Oh, look, here he is now!

(COLONEL enters; SIR JOHN leads the DASHWOODS across stage)

SIR JOHN: This is Colonel Brandon, my very best friend in the entire world.

MARIANNE: You're the park guy!

COLONEL: I am pleased to make your acquaintance.

(to audience) Oh my! I think I'm in love with Marianne!

MARIANNE: *(to ELINOR)* Ewwww, I just heard that old guy say he loves me.

ELINOR: He is not old.

MARIANNE: He is at least 30. Which is ancient... old enough to be my father.

MRS. DASHWOOD: Excuse me, I'm 35. What do you think of me?

MARIANNE: Ummm... did not you hear him complain of the rheumatism?

ELINOR: When did he ever talk about rheumatism?

MARIANNE: Never mind. He totally loves me, and I am not into it.

MRS. DASHWOOD: *(to others)* We better get going. Thank you again for having us!

(ALL exit)

(ELINOR and MRS. DASHWOOD are talking; MARIANNE enters)

MARIANNE: Good Morning! Time to go for a walk! There is so much beauty in the morning light!

ELINOR: Calm down, Marianne.

MARIANNE: I can't calm down!! I have to tell everyone how much I appreciate nature!!

ELINOR: But it looks like it might rain.

MARIANNE: Even better! I'll appreciate the storm! What could possibly go wrong during a walk in the rain!

(MARIANNE exits)

ELINOR: She just jinxed that, didn't she?

MRS. DASHWOOD: Don't be so certain...

(WILLOUGHBY rushes on stage holding MARIANNE in his arms)

WILLOUGHBY: I am Willoughby! The rescuer of this fair lady!

ELINOR: I told you so.

MRS. DASHWOOD: *(gasps)* What happened??

WILLOUGHBY: She was dancing and singing in the rain and twisted her ankle. Thank goodness I was nearby, or she may have died!

(WILLOUGHBY sets MARIANNE down on the couch)

WILLOUGHBY: Marianne, I'm going to check on you every day and you will probably fall in love with me!

MARIANNE: I... I...

WILLOUGHBY: Shhh... don't speak, my dove. I'll see you tomorrow. *(runs offstage yelling)* She almost died! She almost died, and I saved her!

(enter SIR JOHN and COLONEL)

SIR JOHN: Is Marianne okay? I heard she almost died!

ELINOR: It's only a sprained ankle. She's fine.

COLONEL: Marianne, can I get you anything?

ELINOR: She is fine. Everyone, go home now. I will take care of her.

(ALL exit)

ACT 1 SCENE 4

(ELINOR is drawing, MARIANNE reads, and MRS. DASHWOOD plays with a Rubik's Cube)

MARIANNE: Do you think it strange that Edward Ferrars has not come to visit us yet?

ELINOR: He is a busy man.

MRS. DASHWOOD: *(concentrating on cube)* I think he will visit us soon. It is of all things the most natural.

MARIANNE: I just think if he really liked Elinor, he would have come to visit already. At least sent a fruit basket or something.

(MARIANNE moves to the 'window')

ELINOR: Marianne, what are you doing?

MARIANNE: Huh? Nothing. Looking for your Edward and that fruit basket. I'm hungry.

(MARIANNE is staring longingly out the window)

ELINOR: Stop watching for Willoughby.

MARIANNE: What?! I wasn't!

(SERVANT enters)

SERVANT: Mr. Willoughby is here to call on Miss Marianne Dashwood.

(MARIANNE jumps up and squeals with excitement)

ELINOR: Marianne, show some propriety of self-command.

MARIANNE: Elinor, restraining my emotions is not merely an unnecessary effort, but a disgraceful subjection of reason to common-place and mistaken notions.

ELINOR: What?

MARIANNE: If I feel something, I'm going to show it! Love me or leave me, sister!

ELINOR: Oh, brother.

(WILLOUGHBY enters with a flourish and bows; MRS. DASHWOOD hides cube)

WILLOUGHBY: Dear Marianne! I see you are well!

MARIANNE: Yes, thank you. You saved my life!

WILLOUGHBY: It was nothing! And I have a present for you... a horse!

(WILLOUGHBY pulls a stick horse out from behind his back)

MARIANNE: Yay! A horse!! I will call him... Pecan!

ELINOR: Marianne, it is not in our mother's plan to keep any horse.

MARIANNE: Shush. He got me a horse and I want it. Besides, Pecan can hear you. We will ride every day!

WILLOUGHBY: Hurray! I have to go now. Bye!

(WILLOUGHBY exits)

ELINOR: Marianne, you can't accept that horse. He doesn't fit in the house and you barely know this Willoughby guy.

MARIANNE: You are mistaken, Elinor... I am much better acquainted with him, than I am with any other creature in the world, except yourself and mama.

ELINOR: Don't be ridiculous.

(MARIANNE pets the horse; enter SERVANT)

SERVANT: Mr. Edward Ferrars is here to call on Miss Dashwood.

MRS. DASHWOOD: I knew he would come visit!

(ELINOR fixes her hair and smooths her dress; enter EDWARD; SERVANT exits)

EDWARD: Good afternoon, ladies. I am pleased to see you after so long... Marianne, is that a horse?

MARIANNE: *(petting the horse)* Yep!

ELINOR: Hello, Mr. Ferrars. How nice of you to come and visit us!

EDWARD: Thank you for having me. You look beautiful... I MEAN... cool drawing.

ELINOR: You haven't even seen my drawing. But, thank you?

EDWARD: Oh yeah. Totally... I just knew it would be cool.

MRS. DASHWOOD: *(coughing)* How is Mrs. Ferrars, your mom? Has she convinced you to get a job yet?

EDWARD: I have no wish to be distinguished... Thank heaven! I cannot be forced into genius and eloquence.

MARIANNE: *(to herself)* No kidding.

(ELINOR glares at MARIANNE)

MRS. DASHWOOD: You have no ambition, I well know.

MARIANNE: *(muttering under her breath)* You mean he is boring and lazy.

EDWARD: Did you say something, Marianne?

(ELINOR tries to cover up Marianne's rudeness)

ELINOR: Marianne has not shyness to excuse any inattention of hers.

MARIANNE: I don't. What do you think of the village, Mr. Ferrars? Is not the landscape picturesque?

EDWARD: Yeah, it's cool.

MARIANNE: Cool? COOL?! Didn't you notice anything worth admiring?

EDWARD: You must not enquire too far, Marianne—remember I have no knowledge in the picturesque.

MARIANNE: You are so reserved!

EDWARD: Reserved! Am I reserved, Marianne?

MARIANNE: Yes, very.

EDWARD: How, in what manner? What am I to tell you?

MARIANNE: Ughhh! Anything! For Elinor's sake, I am happy you are here. But you have nothing exciting to say!

MRS. DASHWOOD: Marianne!

EDWARD: It's okay. I know Marianne is passionate about everything. I gotta go. Bye.

(EDWARD exits, moping as he goes)

ELINOR: I am going to draw upstairs.

(ELINOR sighs, exits opposite EDWARD)

MRS. DASHWOOD: *(to Marianne)* Now look at what you did.

MARIANNE: And you think it's a bad thing? He's soooo boring!

(ALL exit)

ACT 1 SCENE 5

(MARIANNE and WILLOUGHBY are whispering excitedly; ELINOR is chatting with MRS. DASHWOOD)

SIR JOHN: *(to MRS. DASHWOOD)* I told you I host a lot of cool parties! Oh! I forgot the cookies!

(SIR JOHN exits)

MRS. DASHWOOD: *(loud whispering to ELINOR)* I think Marianne and Mr. Willoughby are in love.

ELINOR: MOM! Have you heard Mr. Willoughby ever actually confess his feelings?

MRS. DASHWOOD: No, but it is obvious.

(ELINOR looks alarmed; she glances over at MARIANNE and WILLOUGHBY; SERVANT enters with a letter on a tray and presents it to WILLOUGHBY who reads it)

WILLOUGHBY: *(standing)* I am now suffering under a very heavy disappointment!

MARIANNE: What's wrong?

WILLOUGHBY: I have to go on business to London.

MRS. DASHWOOD: To London!

MARIANNE: Noooooo!!

(MARIANNE runs offstage crying)

MRS. DASHWOOD: This is very unfortunate.

WILLOUGHBY: I will not torment myself any longer by hanging out with you guys. I will miss you all!

(WILLOUGHBY runs offstage crying)

ELINOR: It is all very strange! So suddenly to be gone!

MRS. DASHWOOD: Willoughby depends on his work. He will not confess to his engagement with Marianne, and will, instead, absent himself from Devonshire for a while.

ELINOR: No! There has been total silence of both on the subject. Neither of them have spoken about an engagement!

(MARIANNE re-enters)

MARIANNE: My life is over! I'll probably never see Willoughby ever again! Ever, ever, EVER!

ELINOR: It's okay. Let's not be too dramatic.

MRS. DASHWOOD: Well, this is a melodrama, and it is Marianne.

MARIANNE: *(still crying)* Yeah. It's the perfect time to be dramatic.

MRS. DASHWOOD: Wait! I have an idea! Why don't you go to London to help Mrs. Jennings pregnant daughter!

ELINOR: I don't know...

MARIANNE: Yes! Yes! It would give me such happiness!

ELINOR: Mama, tell Marianne we cannot go. You need us here.

MRS. DASHWOOD: No, I don't. I am delighted with the plan.

(ALL exit; enter SIR JOHN holding tray of cookies, looking around)

SIR JOHN: What did I miss? *(exits)*

ACT 2 SCENE 1

(MARIANNE and ELINOR enter)

ELINOR: This is a lovely London home.

MARIANNE: I need to write a letter to Willoughby!

(MARIANNE runs offstage; COLONEL enters)

ELINOR: Oh! Colonel, I am monstrous glad to see you... But how did you know we were in town?

COLONEL: I had the pleasure of hearing it where I have been dining. And, well, I'm the Colonel, I know things.

(MARIANNE enters)

MARIANNE: I heard a man's voice! ... Oh. It's just you, Colonel.

COLONEL: Hello, Miss Marianne. It is lovely to see you again.

ELINOR: *(to audience)* Oh my! It looks like Colonel Brandon is as much in love with Marianne as ever!

(MARIANNE and COLONEL both look at ELINOR with wide eyes)

MARIANNE: *(fake coughs; to Elinor)* Has no letter been left here for me?

ELINOR: Marianne, we literally just arrived.

MARIANNE: So what?! Are you certain that no servant... has left any letter?

ELINOR: No.

MARIANNE: What about a carrier pigeon or an owl?

ELINOR: NO. Also... do you actually think mail travels by birds?

MARIANNE: Uhhh...

COLONEL: Anyway... I better get going. I will see all of you soon.

(COLONEL bows and exits)

ELINOR: Colonel Brandon is such a gentleman.

MARIANNE: He is old, and I don't care about him! Where is my sweet Willoughby?!

(MARIANNE runs offstage dramatically)

(enter ELINOR, SIR JOHN, MARIANNE, and any other party-goers that want to join onstage)

SIR JOHN: I cannot think of a better way to spend an evening than with nearly twenty young people, and to amuse them with a ball.

(everyone pairs off in groups and chat; enter COLONEL)

COLONEL: Elinor! I must speak with you!

ELINOR: What's wrong??

COLONEL: Your sister's engagement to Mr. Willoughby is very generally known.

ELINOR: What is going on?! It cannot be generally known, for her own family do not know it.

(enter WILLOUGHBY; MARIANNE runs up to ELINOR)

MARIANNE: Good heavens! He is there—he is there!

(ELINOR shakes MARIANNE by the shoulders)

ELINOR: Pray, pray be composed, and do not betray what you feel to everybody present.

MARIANNE: Go to him, Elinor, and force him to come to me.

(WILLOUGHBY walks over)

ELINOR: Too late. Here he comes.

(ALL step back and watch WILLOUGHBY and MARIANNE speak to each other; SIR JOHN subtly exits if doubling as SERVANT)

WILLOUGHBY: Hello, Marianne.

MARIANNE: Hello, Willoughby.

WILLOUGHBY: I heard you were in town. I tried to call on you.

MARIANNE: I was hoping you would. There is something I have to tell you!

WILLOUGHBY: Me too!

(WILLOUGHBY and MARIANNE speak at the same time)

WILLOUGHBY: I'm engaged!

MARIANNE: I love you!

(ALL gasp)

MARIANNE: What? You're engaged? To me, right? Everyone keeps saying you are engaged to me.

WILLOUGHBY: Awkward... ummm... no. I am engaged to Miss Grey.

MARIANNE: Miss Grey? Who's Miss Grey?

WILLOUGHBY: A lady I met in town.

MARIANNE: Oh, well that's just fantastic!

WILLOUGHBY: My dear Madam... if I have been so unfortunate as to give rise to a belief of more than I felt, I am truly sorry.

MARIANNE: A rise to a belief? We are practically soul mates. You love me.

WILLOUGHBY: *(in a loud whisper to MARIANNE)* Okay, yes. I am in love with you. But I'm poor and have to marry Miss Grey for her money. I'm sorry, Marianne. Goodbye forever.

(WILLOUGHBY exits; MARIANNE looks around)

ELINOR: Marianne, let me take you back...

MARIANNE: No, no, misery such as mine has no pride. I care not who knows that I am wretched.

(MARIANNE sobs melodramatically as she and ELINOR walk offstage; ALL exit)

(ELINOR sits alone, reading; enter COLONEL)

COLONEL: Miss Dashwood, there is something I must tell you. Mr. Willoughby is not a nice man! He proposed to my adopted daughter and then abandoned her!

ELINOR: Oh my! And you are afraid that this might happen to Marianne.

COLONEL: Precisely. His character is now before you.

ELINOR: Thank you for telling me.

COLONEL: Use your own discretion however, in communicating to Marianne what I have told you.

(COLONEL bows to ELINOR; ALL exit)

ACT 2 SCENE 4

(enter ELINOR and MARIANNE)

MARIANNE: *(to audience)* This play is lasting quite long, we must wrap it up. *(to ELINOR)* Elinor! Lucy Steele and Edward Ferrars are secretly engaged!

ELINOR: How did you hear that?? And who is Lucy?

MARIANNE: A random friend of yours.

ELINOR: Some friend!

MARIANNE: Apparently, Mr. Ferrars' family does not approve of their engagement and they disowned him.

(COLONEL enters)

COLONEL: Wait! I will be his patron, and he can work near my estate!

(EDWARD enters)

EDWARD: Thank you so much, Colonel! But, Lucy just dumped me to marry my brother. Because, he inherits our family wealth and I'll be poor.

COLONEL: That stinks.

EDWARD: Yes, but now I can marry my one true love! Elinor, will you marry me??

ELINOR: Yes!!

MARIANNE: Wait a minute. *(pulling ELINOR aside)* Elinor, don't you find it odd that he only chose you after Lucy rejected him?

ELINOR: Nope! He is a man of honor!

MARIANNE: Right...

ELINOR: Well, now I wish you had someone to marry, Marianne.

(COLONEL coughs to get their attention)

ELINOR: Wait! You can marry Colonel Brandon so that we can all live near each other!

MARIANNE: Sure, why not! I have matured a lot and realize that Willoughby wasn't right for me.

COLONEL: Score!

(MRS. DASHWOOD enters)

MRS. DASHWOOD: I seem to have missed something.

ELINOR: We are getting married!

MRS. DASHWOOD: Hurray! We won't die of poverty! What a wonderful ending! Oh, and I get grandkids, too! Let's go celebrate!

(ELINOR and MARIANNE look at each other with shocked eyes as MRS. DASHWOOD locks arms with girls and dances offstage)

THE END

The 20-Minute or so
Sense & Sensibility
for Kids

by Jane Austen
Creatively modified by
Amanda Thayer & Brendan P. Kelso
9-12 Actors
CAST OF CHARACTERS:

ELINOR: older Dashwood sister; needs to be in control; the one with sense

MARIANNE: younger Dashwood sister; loves emotion and attention; the one with sensibility

MRS. DASHWOOD: Dashwood mother; kind of kooky.

[1]**DAD:** dead dad

EDWARD: awkward friend of the Dashwood sisters; secretly in love with Elinor

WILLOUGHBY: loves Marianne but must marry someone else because he is poor

COLONEL: friend of Sir John; also in love with Marianne

[1]**SIR JOHN:** cousin of Mrs. Dashwood; very excited about everything all the time

MRS. JENNINGS: jolly mother-in-law of Sir John

[2]**MRS. JOHN DW:** daughter-in-law to Mrs. Dashwood

[2]**LUCY:** secret fiance of Edward

[1]**SERVANT:** butler at various estates

The same actors can play the following parts:

[1]DAD, SERVANT, and SIR JOHN

[2]LUCY and MRS. JOHN DW

(enter MRS. DASHWOOD)

MRS. DASHWOOD: Girls, come in here!

(enter ELINOR and MARIANNE)

MRS. DASHWOOD: Where's your sister?

MARIANNE: She got cut from the play.

MRS. DASHWOOD: What?!

ELINOR: She missed a bunch of rehearsals, small part, director let her go. But more importantly, mother, are you okay?

MRS. DASHWOOD: Me? I'm fine. Buuuut... your father's dead.

MARIANNE: What?! Nooooo! Dad!!!

DAD: *(offstage)* Sorry girls!

ELINOR: Poor Dad! Mom, can I get you anything? Lavender drops? Warm socks? Some chocolate cake?

MRS. DASHWOOD: You are always trying to comfort everyone, Elinor.

ELINOR: It's what I do.

MRS. DASHWOOD: Anyway, now we're super poor. Your brother and nephew inherited everything.

MARIANNE: What?! Nooooo! Dad!!!

DAD: *(offstage)* Again, sorry girls!

MARIANNE: Great. Another loss for women.

ELINOR: NO ONE PANIC! *(She pulls out a binder)*

MARIANNE: I'm not panicked. What have wealth or grandeur to do with happiness?

ELINOR: *(flipping through binder)* Everything? I have a plan for this exact situation. *(stops and points to a page)* Here we go! We all live together until men marry us and save us from poverty!

MARIANNE: Oh joy. I can't wait to be saved by a man.

MRS. DASHWOOD: *(to audience)* If you haven't figured it out yet, *(points at ELINOR)* the one with sense, *(to MARIANNE)* and sensibility.

(SERVANT enters)

SERVANT: Mr. Edward Ferrars is here to call on Miss Dashwood. *(exits)*

MARIANNE & MRS. DASHWOOD: Oooooooooh!

(enter EDWARD FERRARS)

EDWARD: Oh, hey, Elinor. Want to go for a walk or whatever? I'm not good with words. That's why I'm handsome.

ELINOR: Okay!

(exit ELINOR and EDWARD)

MARIANNE & MRS. DASHWOOD: Oooooooooh!

MRS. DASHWOOD: In a few months, my dear Marianne, Elinor will marry Edward and save us all. At least *she* will be happy.

MARIANNE: Meh. Edward is very amiable... But he is NOT handsome. And he has no real taste in art.

MRS. DASHWOOD: What does handsome have to do with love?

MARIANNE: Please mother, you're embarrassing yourself. *(motions to audience)*

MRS. DASHWOOD: He always admires Elinor's drawings very much.

MARIANNE: He admires the drawings because he likes her, not as a connoisseur. I'll never find someone to love. I require so much!

MRS. DASHWOOD: You do, Marianne. But, you aren't even seventeen. It is yet too early in life to despair of such a happiness. You can start despairing when you are twenty-one. That's when you will be an old maid.

MARIANNE: Gee, thanks, Mom.

(MARIANNE rolls her eyes; enter SERVANT)

SERVANT: Mrs. Dashwood is here to see Mrs. Dashwood. *(exits)*

(MARIANNE and MRS. DASHWOOD look at each other, confused; enter MRS. JOHN DASHWOOD)

MRS. JOHN DW: I'm moving in.

MRS. DASHWOOD: Into my house?

MRS. JOHN DW: Well, technically, this is my house now. Your stepson is the only boy, he inherited the house. So, bye-bye!

MRS. DASHWOOD: Right. Good. Thanks for the reminder.

(enter SERVANT holding a letter on a tray)

SERVANT: A letter for Mrs. Dashwood.

(both MRS. DASHWOOD and MRS. JOHN DASHWOOD reach for letter)

MRS. JOHN DW: I am Mrs. Dashwood.

MRS. DASHWOOD: No, I am Mrs. Dashwood. You are Mrs. JOHN Dashwood.

MRS. JOHN DW: But your husband is dead. Which makes my husband, your stepson, the only Mr. Dashwood. Which makes me the real Mrs. Dashwood.

SERVANT: This is too confusing. Will the real Mrs. Dashwood please stand up?

(both MRS. DASHWOOD and MRS. JOHN DASHWOOD stand up; they glare at each other; SERVANT sighs and does "eenie-meenie-miney-mo" to determine; he lands on MRS. DASHWOOD)

MRS. DASHWOOD: Yes! I win! I mean… thank you for the letter. You may go. *(SERVANT exits)* Oh! It is a letter from my cousin! He is giving us a cottage to live in now that you have stolen our house. Thief!

MRS. JOHN DW: Oh goody. When can you leave? Oh, I know, how about… NOW!

(MRS. DASHWOOD sticks her tongue at MRS. JOHN DW; enter EDWARD and ELINOR, returning from their walk)

MRS. DASHWOOD: *(perusing letter)* We are moving to Devonshire!

EDWARD: Devonshire! Are you, indeed, going there? So far from hence!

MRS. DASHWOOD: It is but a cottage… but I hope to see many of my friends in it. *(looking at Edward)*

ELINOR: *(to audience)* I must now hide my sadness about leaving the person I am in love with. Hmmm, I know! *(to MRS. DASHWOOD)* We better get packing!

(ALL exit)

(enter SIR JOHN; opposite ELINOR, MARIANNE, MRS. DASHWOOD)

SIR JOHN: Hello!! Welcome! I am Sir John, and I am excited about everything, all the time! *(randomly points around)* Here is the cottage. Here are the gardens. That big place over there is my house. Now you have seen everything! Isn't it wonderful??

MRS. DASHWOOD: Thank you for having us, Sir John.

SIR JOHN: Buckle up! You ladies are about to be totally social. I am forever forming parties to eat cold ham and chicken out of doors, and in winter I host loads of private balls.

MRS. DASHWOOD: You hear that, girls? So social!

SIR JOHN: However, you will only see one gentleman here besides myself. He is a particular friend who is staying at the park.

MARIANNE: At the park? Is he homeless? A poet? An artist? Does he appreciate nature? Why does he live in a park?

ELINOR: *(coughs)* We look forward to meeting your friend.

SIR JOHN: Great! Oh, look, here he is with my family!

(MRS. JENNINGS and COLONEL enter; SIR JOHN leads the DASHWOODS across stage)

SIR JOHN: This is Mrs. Jennings, my mother-in-law; and Colonel Brandon, my very best friend in the entire world.

MARIANNE: You're the park guy!

COLONEL: I am pleased to make your acquaintance.

MRS. JENNINGS: What lovely daughters you have, Mrs. Dashwood! I am sure they will both be married by the end of the month.

MARIANNE: Whoa, slow down there.

COLONEL: *(to audience)* Oh my! I think I'm in love with Marianne!

MARIANNE: *(to ELINOR)* Ewwww, I just heard that old guy say he loves me.

ELINOR: He is not old.

MARIANNE: He is at least 30. Which is ancient... old enough to be my father.

MRS. DASHWOOD: Excuse me, I'm 35. What do you think of me?

MARIANNE: Ummm... did not you hear him complain of the rheumatism?

ELINOR: When did he ever talk about rheumatism?

MARIANNE: Never mind. He totally loves me, and I am not into it.

MRS. DASHWOOD: *(to others)* We better get going. Thank you again for having us!

(ALL exit)

ACT 1 SCENE 3

*(ELINOR and MRS. DASHWOOD are talking;
MARIANNE enters)*

MARIANNE: Good Morning! Time to go for a walk!
There is so much beauty in the morning light!

ELINOR: Calm down, Marianne.

MARIANNE: I can't calm down!! I have to tell
everyone how much I appreciate nature!!

ELINOR: But it looks like it might rain.

MARIANNE: Even better! I'll appreciate the storm!
What could possibly go wrong during a walk in the
rain!

(MARIANNE exits)

ELINOR: She just jinxed that, didn't she?

MRS. DASHWOOD: Don't be so certain...

*(WILLOUGHBY rushes on stage holding MARIANNE in
his arms)*

WILLOUGHBY: I am Willoughby! The rescuer of this
fair lady!

ELINOR: I told you so.

MRS. DASHWOOD: *(gasps)* What happened??

WILLOUGHBY: She was dancing and singing in the rain and twisted her ankle. Thank goodness I was nearby, or she may have died!

(WILLOUGHBY sets MARIANNE down on the couch)

WILLOUGHBY: Marianne, I'm going to check on you every day and you will probably fall in love with me!

MARIANNE: I... I...

WILLOUGHBY: Shhh... don't speak, my dove. I'll see you tomorrow. *(runs offstage yelling)* She almost died! She almost died, and I saved her!

(enter SIR JOHN, COLONEL, and MRS. JENNINGS)

MRS. JENNINGS: Is Marianne okay? I heard she almost died!

ELINOR: It's only a sprained ankle, Mrs. Jennings. She's fine.

COLONEL: Marianne, can I get you anything?

ELINOR: She is fine. Everyone, go home now. I will take care of her.

(ALL exit)

(ELINOR is drawing, MARIANNE reads, and MRS. DASHWOOD plays with a Rubik's Cube; SERVANT crosses with a sign that says, "The next day")

MARIANNE: Do you think it strange that Edward Ferrars has not come to visit us yet?

ELINOR: He is a busy man.

MRS. DASHWOOD: *(concentrating on cube)* I think he will visit us soon. It is of all things the most natural.

MARIANNE: I just think if he really liked Elinor, he would have come to visit already. At least sent a fruit basket or something.

(MARIANNE moves to the 'window')

ELINOR: Marianne, what are you doing?

MARIANNE: Huh? Nothing. Looking for your Edward and that fruit basket. I'm hungry.

(MARIANNE is staring longingly out the window)

ELINOR: Stop watching for Willoughby.

MARIANNE: What?! I wasn't!

(SERVANT enters)

SERVANT: Mr. Willoughby is here to call on Miss Marianne Dashwood.

(MARIANNE jumps up and squeals with excitement)

ELINOR: Marianne, show some propriety of self-command.

MARIANNE: Elinor, restraining my emotions is not merely an unnecessary effort, but a disgraceful subjection of reason to common-place and mistaken notions.

ELINOR: What?

MARIANNE: If I feel something, I'm going to show it! Love me or leave me, sister!

ELINOR: Oh, brother.

(WILLOUGHBY enters with a flourish and bows; MRS. DASHWOOD hides cube)

WILLOUGHBY: Dear Marianne! I see you are well!

MARIANNE: Yes, thank you. You saved my life!

WILLOUGHBY: It was nothing! And I have a present for you... a horse!

(WILLOUGHBY pulls a stick horse out from behind his back)

MARIANNE: Yay! A horse!! I will call him... Pecan!

ELINOR: Marianne, it is not in our mother's plan to keep any horse.

MARIANNE: Shush. He got me a horse and I want it. Besides, Pecan can hear you. We will ride every day!

WILLOUGHBY: Hurray! I have to go now. Bye!

(exit WILLOUGHBY)

ELINOR: Marianne, you can't accept that horse. He doesn't fit in the house and you barely know this Willoughby guy.

MARIANNE: You are mistaken, Elinor... I am much better acquainted with him, than I am with any other creature in the world, except yourself and mama.

ELINOR: Don't be ridiculous.

(MARIANNE pets the horse; enter SERVANT)

SERVANT: Mr. Edward Ferrars is here to call on Miss Dashwood.

MRS. DASHWOOD: I knew he would come visit!

(ELINOR fixes her hair and smooths her dress; enter EDWARD; SERVANT exits)

EDWARD: Good afternoon, ladies. I am pleased to see you after so long... Marianne, is that a horse?

MARIANNE: *(petting the horse)* Yep!

ELINOR: Hello, Mr. Ferrars. How nice of you to come and visit us!

EDWARD: Thank you for having me. You look beautiful... I MEAN... cool drawing.

ELINOR: You haven't even seen my drawing. But, thank you?

EDWARD: Oh yeah. Totally... I just knew it would be cool.

MRS. DASHWOOD: *(coughing)* How is Mrs. Ferrars, your mom? Has she convinced you to get a job yet?

EDWARD: I have no wish to be distinguished... Thank heaven! I cannot be forced into genius and eloquence.

MARIANNE: *(to herself)* No kidding.

(ELINOR glares at MARIANNE)

MRS. DASHWOOD: You have no ambition, I well know.

MARIANNE: *(muttering under her breath)* You mean he is boring and lazy.

EDWARD: Did you say something, Marianne?

(ELINOR tries to cover up Marianne's rudeness)

ELINOR: Marianne has not shyness to excuse any inattention of hers.

MARIANNE: I don't. What do you think of the village, Mr. Ferrars? Is not the landscape picturesque?

EDWARD: Yeah, it's cool.

MARIANNE: Cool? COOL?! Didn't you notice anything worth admiring?

EDWARD: You must not enquire too far, Marianne—remember I have no knowledge in the picturesque.

MARIANNE: You are so reserved!

EDWARD: Reserved! Am I reserved, Marianne?

MARIANNE: Yes, very.

EDWARD: How, in what manner? What am I to tell you?

MARIANNE: Ughhh! Anything! For Elinor's sake, I am happy you are here. But you have nothing exciting to say!

MRS. DASHWOOD: Marianne!

EDWARD: It's okay. I know Marianne is passionate about everything. I gotta go. Bye.

(EDWARD exits, moping as he goes)

ELINOR: I am going to draw upstairs.

(ELINOR sighs, exits opposite EDWARD)

MRS. DASHWOOD: *(to Marianne)* Now look at what you did.

MARIANNE: And you think it's a bad thing? He's soooo boring!

(ALL exit)

(MARIANNE and WILLOUGHBY are whispering excitedly; ELINOR is chatting with MRS. DASHWOOD and MRS. JENNINGS)

SIR JOHN: *(to MRS. DASHWOOD)* I told you I host a lot of cool parties! Oh! I forgot the cookies!

(SIR JOHN exits)

MRS. JENNINGS: *(loud whispering to ELINOR)* I think Marianne and Mr. Willoughby are in love.

ELINOR: Mrs. Jennings! Have you heard Mr. Willoughby ever actually confess his feelings?

MRS. JENNINGS: No, but it is obvious.

(ELINOR looks alarmed; she glances over at MARIANNE and WILLOUGHBY; SERVANT enters with a letter on a tray and presents it to WILLOUGHBY who reads it)

WILLOUGHBY: *(standing)* I am now suffering under a very heavy disappointment!

MARIANNE: What's wrong?

WILLOUGHBY: I have to go on business to London.

MRS. DASHWOOD: To London!

MARIANNE: Nooooooo!!

(MARIANNE runs offstage crying)

MRS. DASHWOOD: This is very unfortunate.

WILLOUGHBY: I will not torment myself any longer by hanging out with you guys. I will miss you all!

(WILLOUGHBY runs offstage crying)

ELINOR: It is all very strange! So suddenly to be gone!

MRS. DASHWOOD: Willoughby depends on his work. He will not confess to his engagement with Marianne, and will, instead, absent himself from Devonshire for a while.

MRS. JENNINGS: So, you think they are engaged too??

MRS. DASHWOOD: Oh, totally!

ELINOR: No! There has been total silence of both on the subject. Neither of them have spoken about an engagement!

(MARIANNE re-enters)

MARIANNE: My life is over! I'll probably never see Willoughby ever again! Ever, ever, EVER!

ELINOR: It's okay. Let's not be too dramatic.

MRS. DASHWOOD: Well, this is a melodrama, and it is Marianne.

MARIANNE: *(still crying)* Yeah. It's the perfect time to be dramatic.

MRS. JENNINGS: Wait! I have an idea! I am heading to London to help my pregnant daughter! Would you ladies like to accompany me?

ELINOR: I don't know...

MARIANNE: Yes! Yes! It would give me such happiness to be able to accept your invitation!

ELINOR: Mama, tell Marianne we cannot go. You need us here.

MRS. DASHWOOD: No, I don't. I am delighted with the plan.

MRS. JENNINGS: Good! Then it's settled!

(ALL exit; enter SIR JOHN holding tray of cookies, looking around)

SIR JOHN: What did I miss? *(exits)*

ACT 2 SCENE 1

(MRS. JENNINGS, MARIANNE, and ELINOR enter)

ELINOR: You have a lovely London home, Mrs. Jennings.

MARIANNE: I need to write a letter to Willoughby!

(MARIANNE runs offstage; SERVANT enters)

SERVANT: There is a Colonel Brandon here.

(COLONEL enters)

MRS. JENNINGS: Oh! Colonel, I am monstrous glad to see you... But how did you know we were in town?

COLONEL: I had the pleasure of hearing it at your daughter's, where I have been dining.

MRS. JENNINGS: Oh! You did; How does my super pregnant daughter Charlotte do?

COLONEL: Mrs. Palmer appeared quite well... rounded.

(MARIANNE enters)

MARIANNE: I heard a man's voice! ... Oh. It's just you, Colonel.

COLONEL: Hello, Miss Marianne. It is lovely to see you again.

MRS. JENNINGS: Oh my! It looks like Colonel Brandon is as much in love with Marianne as ever!

(MARIANNE and COLONEL both look at MRS. JENNINGS with wide eyes; ELINOR smacks her hand against her forehead)

MARIANNE: *(to Elinor)* Has no letter been left here for me?

ELINOR: Marianne, we literally just arrived.

MARIANNE: So what?! Are you certain that no servant... has left any letter?

ELINOR: No.

MARIANNE: What about a carrier pigeon or an owl?

ELINOR: NO. Also... do you actually think mail travels by birds?

MARIANNE: Uhhh...

COLONEL: Anyway... I better get going. I will see all of you soon.

(COLONEL bows and exits)

ELINOR: Colonel Brandon is such a gentleman.

MARIANNE: He is old, and I don't care about him! Where is my sweet Willoughby?!

(MARIANNE runs offstage dramatically)

ACT 2 SCENE 2

(enter ELINOR, SIR JOHN, MARIANNE, MRS. JENNINGS, and any other party-goers that want to join onstage)

SIR JOHN: I cannot think of a better way to spend an evening than with nearly twenty young people, and to amuse them with a ball.

(everyone pairs off in groups and chat; enter COLONEL)

COLONEL: Elinor! I must speak with you!

ELINOR: What's wrong??

COLONEL: Your sister's engagement to Mr. Willoughby is very generally known.

ELINOR: What is going on?! It cannot be generally known, for her own family do not know it.

(enter WILLOUGHBY; MARIANNE runs up to ELINOR)

MARIANNE: Good heavens! He is there–he is there!

(ELINOR shakes MARIANNE by the shoulders)

ELINOR: Pray, pray be composed, and do not betray what you feel to everybody present.

MARIANNE: Go to him, Elinor, and force him to come to me.

(WILLOUGHBY walks over)

ELINOR: Too late. Here he comes.

(ALL step back and watch WILLOUGHBY and MARIANNE speak to each other; SIR JOHN subtly exits if doubling as SERVANT)

WILLOUGHBY: Hello, Marianne.

MARIANNE: Hello, Willoughby.

WILLOUGHBY: I heard you were in town. I tried to call on you.

MARIANNE: I was hoping you would. There is something I have to tell you!

WILLOUGHBY: Me too!

(WILLOUGHBY and MARIANNE speak at the same time)

WILLOUGHBY: I'm engaged!

MARIANNE: I love you!

(ALL gasp)

MARIANNE: What? You're engaged? To me, right? Everyone keeps saying you are engaged to me.

WILLOUGHBY: Awkward... ummm... no. I am engaged to Miss Grey.

MARIANNE: Miss Grey? Who's Miss Grey?

WILLOUGHBY: A lady I met in town.

MARIANNE: Oh, well that's just fantastic!

WILLOUGHBY: My dear Madam... if I have been so unfortunate as to give rise to a belief of more than I felt, I am truly sorry.

MARIANNE: A rise to a belief? We are practically soul mates. You love me.

WILLOUGHBY: *(in a loud whisper to MARIANNE)* Okay, yes. I am in love with you. But I'm poor and have to marry Miss Grey for her money.

WILLOUGHBY: I'm sorry, Marianne. Goodbye forever.

(WILLOUGHBY exits; MARIANNE looks around)

ELINOR: Marianne, let me take you back...

MARIANNE: No, no, misery such as mine has no pride. I care not who knows that I am wretched.

(MARIANNE sobs melodramatically as she and ELINOR walk offstage; ALL exit)

(ELINOR sits alone, reading; enter SERVANT)

SERVANT: Colonel Brandon is here to see Miss Dashwood.

(COLONEL enters; SERVANT exits)

COLONEL: Miss Dashwood, there is something I must tell you. Mr. Willoughby is not a nice man! He proposed to my adopted daughter and then abandoned her!

ELINOR: Oh my! And you are afraid that this might happen to Marianne.

COLONEL: Precisely. His character is now before you.

ELINOR: Thank you for telling me.

COLONEL: Use your own discretion however, in communicating to Marianne what I have told you.

(COLONEL bows to ELINOR and exits; enter SERVANT)

SERVANT: There is a Miss Lucy Steele here to see Miss Dashwood.

ELINOR: Who?

(LUCY enters; SERVANT exits)

LUCY: Elinor, my very close friend, I must speak with you!

ELINOR: Do I know you?

LUCY: Yes of course! In an earlier part of the book, we established our friendship, but that scene was cut for time in this adaptation. See, right here. *(shows ELINOR pages in Sense & Sensibility book)*

ELINOR: Oh! That's right! *(to audience)* I actually find her quite annoying, but I am too nice to say anything.

LUCY: I can still hear you.

ELINOR: Oh, sorry. Go on.

LUCY: I simply must talk with you. I have a big, fat depressing secret... I am in love.

ELINOR: That's nice. With whom?

LUCY: Mr. Edward Ferrars! You know him, right?

ELINOR: You mean the man that I am also secretly in love with?

LUCY: What was that?

ELINOR: *(eyes wide)* Oh. Nothing. Uh... wow! So, you love Edward Ferrars!

LUCY: Yes! And not only am I in love... we have been engaged these four years.

ELINOR: Four years? Engaged?! I did not know that you were even acquainted.

LUCY: No one knows. And heaven knows how much longer we may have to wait to get married. Now you can feel miserable with me!

ELINOR: Great.

LUCY: Phew! I feel so much better now that you are sharing in my misery. I'll see you later!

(LUCY exits)

ELINOR: Why does everyone keep telling me their depressing secrets!

(ELINOR exits)

(enter MRS. JENNINGS, ELINOR, and MARIANNE)

MRS. JENNINGS: *(to audience)* This play is lasting quite long, we must wrap it up. *(to ELINOR)* Elinor! Lucy Steele and Edward Ferrars are secretly engaged!

ELINOR: How did you hear that?? Were you listening at the door?

MRS. JENNINGS: No! I heard it somewhere else. Apparently, Mr. Ferrars' family does not approve of their engagement and they disowned him.

(COLONEL enters)

COLONEL: Wait! I will be his patron, and he can work near my estate!

(EDWARD and LUCY enter)

EDWARD: Thank you so much, Colonel! Lucy, we will be poor, but now we have a place to live and we can get married!

LUCY: To me? No money? No thanks. I'll marry your brother instead since he will now inherit your family wealth. You can go be poor with what's-her-name.

(LUCY exits)

EDWARD: That stinks... but now I can marry my one true love! Elinor, will you marry me??

ELINOR: Yes!!

MARIANNE: Wait a minute. *(pulling ELINOR aside)* Elinor, don't you find it odd that he only chose you after Lucy rejected him?

ELINOR: Nope! He is a man of honor!

MARIANNE: Right...

ELINOR: Well, now I wish you had someone to marry, Marianne.

(COLONEL coughs to get their attention)

ELINOR: Wait! You can marry Colonel Brandon so that we can all live near each other!

MARIANNE: Sure, why not! I have matured a lot and realize that Willoughby wasn't right for me.

COLONEL: Score!

(MRS. DASHWOOD enters)

MRS. DASHWOOD: I seem to have missed something.

ELINOR: We are getting married!

MRS. DASHWOOD: Hurray! We won't die of poverty! What a wonderful ending! Oh, and I get grandkids, too! Let's go celebrate!

(ELINOR and MARIANNE look at each other with shocked eyes as MRS. DASHWOOD locks arms with girls and dances offstage)

THE END

NOTES

The 25-Minute or so
Sense & Sensibility
for Kids

by Jane Austen
Creatively modified by
Amanda Thayer & Brendan P. Kelso
11-15 Actors
CAST OF CHARACTERS:

ELINOR: older Dashwood sister; needs to be in control; the one with sense

MARIANNE: younger Dashwood sister; loves emotion and attention; the one with sensibility

MRS. DASHWOOD: Dashwood mother; kind of kooky.

[1]**DAD:** dead dad

EDWARD: awkward friend of the Dashwood sisters; secretly in love with Elinor

WILLOUGHBY: loves Marianne but must marry someone else because he is poor

COLONEL: friend of Sir John; also in love with Marianne

[1]**SIR JOHN:** cousin of Mrs. Dashwood; very excited about everything all the time

[3]**LADY MIDDLETON:** wife of Sir John; very snooty

MRS. JENNINGS: jolly mother-in-law of Sir John

[4]**MRS. PALMER:** pregnant daughter of Mrs. Jennings

[2]**MRS. JOHN DW:** daughter-in-law to Mrs. Dashwood

[3]**MISS GREY:** new fiance of Willoughby

[2]**LUCY:** secret fiance of Edward

[4]**SERVANT:** butler at various estates

The same actors can play the following parts:
[1]DAD and SIR JOHN
[2]LUCY and MRS. JOHN DW
[3]LADY MIDDLETON and MRS GREY
[4]SERVANT and MRS. PALMER

ACT 1 SCENE 1

(enter MRS. DASHWOOD)

MRS. DASHWOOD: Girls, come in here!

(enter ELINOR and MARIANNE)

MRS. DASHWOOD: Where's your sister?

MARIANNE: She got cut from the play.

MRS. DASHWOOD: What?!

ELINOR: She missed a bunch of rehearsals, small part, director let her go. But more importantly, mother, are you okay?

MRS. DASHWOOD: Me? I'm fine. Buuuut... your father's dead.

MARIANNE: What?! Nooooo! Dad!!!

DAD: *(offstage)* Sorry girls!

ELINOR: Poor Dad! Mom, can I get you anything? Lavender drops? Warm socks? Some chocolate cake?

MRS. DASHWOOD: You are always trying to comfort everyone, Elinor.

ELINOR: It's what I do.

MRS. DASHWOOD: Anyway, now we're super poor. Your brother and nephew inherited everything.

MARIANNE: What?! Nooooo! Dad!!!

DAD: *(offstage)* Again, sorry girls!

MARIANNE: Great. Another loss for women.

ELINOR: NO ONE PANIC! *(She pulls out a binder)*

MARIANNE: I'm not panicked. What have wealth or grandeur to do with happiness?

ELINOR: *(flipping through binder)* Everything? I have a plan for this exact situation. *(stops and points to a page)* Here we go! We all live together until men marry us and save us from poverty!

MARIANNE: Oh joy. I can't wait to be saved by a man.

MRS. DASHWOOD: *(to audience)* If you haven't figured it out yet, *(points at ELINOR)* the one with sense, *(to MARIANNE)* and sensibility.

(SERVANT enters)

SERVANT: Mr. Edward Ferrars is here to call on Miss Dashwood. *(exits)*

MARIANNE & MRS. DASHWOOD: Ooooooooooh!

(enter EDWARD FERRARS)

EDWARD: Oh, hey, Elinor. Want to go for a walk or whatever? I'm not good with words. That's why I'm handsome.

ELINOR: Okay!

(exit ELINOR and EDWARD)

MARIANNE & MRS. DASHWOOD: Ooooooooooh!

MRS. DASHWOOD: In a few months, my dear Marianne, Elinor will marry Edward and save us all. At least *she* will be happy.

MARIANNE: Meh. Edward is very amiable... But he is NOT handsome. And he has no real taste in art.

MRS. DASHWOOD: What does handsome have to do with love?

MARIANNE: Please mother, you're embarrassing yourself. *(motions to audience)*

MRS. DASHWOOD: He always admires Elinor's drawings very much.

MARIANNE: He admires the drawings because he likes her, not as a connoisseur. I'll never find someone to love. I require so much!

MRS. DASHWOOD: You do, Marianne. But, you aren't even seventeen. It is yet too early in life to despair of such a happiness. You can start despairing when you are twenty-one. That's when you will be an old maid.

MARIANNE: Gee, thanks, Mom.

(MARIANNE rolls her eyes; enter SERVANT)

SERVANT: Mrs. Dashwood is here to see Mrs. Dashwood. *(exits)*

(MARIANNE and MRS. DASHWOOD look at each other, confused; enter MRS. JOHN DASHWOOD)

MRS. JOHN DW: I'm moving in.

MRS. DASHWOOD: Into my house?

MRS. JOHN DW: Well, technically, this is my house now. Your stepson is the only boy, he inherited the house. So, bye-bye!

MRS. DASHWOOD: Right. Good. Thanks for the reminder.

(enter SERVANT holding a letter on a tray)

SERVANT: A letter for Mrs. Dashwood.

(both MRS. DASHWOOD and MRS. JOHN DASHWOOD reach for letter)

MRS. JOHN DW: I am Mrs. Dashwood.

MRS. DASHWOOD: No, I am Mrs. Dashwood. You are Mrs. JOHN Dashwood.

MRS. JOHN DW: But your husband is dead. Which makes my husband, your stepson, the only Mr. Dashwood. Which makes me the real Mrs. Dashwood.

SERVANT: This is too confusing. Will the real Mrs. Dashwood please stand up?

(both MRS. DASHWOOD and MRS. JOHN DASHWOOD stand up; they glare at each other; SERVANT sighs and does "eenie-meenie-miney-mo" to determine; he lands on MRS. DASHWOOD)

MRS. DASHWOOD: Yes! I win! I mean... thank you for the letter. You may go. *(SERVANT exits)* Oh! It is a letter from my cousin! He is giving us a cottage to live in now that you have stolen our house. Thief!

MRS. JOHN DW: Oh goody. When can you leave? Oh, I know, how about... NOW!

(MRS. DASHWOOD sticks her tongue at MRS. JOHN DW; enter EDWARD and ELINOR, returning from their walk)

MRS. DASHWOOD: *(perusing letter)* We are moving to Devonshire!

EDWARD: Devonshire! Are you, indeed, going there? So far from hence!

MRS. DASHWOOD: It is but a cottage... but I hope to see many of my friends in it. *(looking at Edward)*

ELINOR: *(to audience)* I must now hide my sadness about leaving the person I am in love with. Hmmm, I know! *(to MRS. DASHWOOD)* We better get packing!

(ALL exit)

<h1 style="text-align:center">ACT 1 SCENE 2</h1>

(enter SIR JOHN; opposite ELINOR, MARIANNE, MRS. DASHWOOD)

SIR JOHN: Hello!! Welcome! I am Sir John, and I am excited about everything, all the time! *(randomly points around)* Here is the cottage. Here are the gardens. That big place over there is my house. Now you have seen everything! Isn't it wonderful??

MRS. DASHWOOD: Thank you for having us, Sir John.

SIR JOHN: Buckle up! You ladies are about to be totally social. I am forever forming parties to eat cold ham and chicken out of doors, and in winter I host loads of private balls.

MRS. DASHWOOD: You hear that, girls? So social!

SIR JOHN: However, you will only see one gentleman here besides myself. He is a particular friend who is staying at the park.

MARIANNE: At the park? Is he homeless? A poet? An artist? Does he appreciate nature? Why does he live in a park?

ELINOR: *(coughs)* We look forward to meeting your friend.

SIR JOHN: Great! Oh, look, here he is with my family!

(LADY MIDDLETON, MRS. JENNINGS, and COLONEL enter; SIR JOHN leads the DASHWOODS across stage)

SIR JOHN: This is Lady Middleton, my beautiful wife; Mrs. Jennings, my mother-in-law; and Colonel Brandon, my very best friend in the entire world.

MARIANNE: You're the park guy!

COLONEL: I am pleased to make your acquaintance.

LADY MIDDLETON: Nice to meet you, too.

MRS. JENNINGS: What lovely daughters you have, Mrs. Dashwood! I am sure they will both be married by the end of the month.

MARIANNE: Whoa, slow down there.

COLONEL: *(to audience)* Oh my! I think I'm in love with Marianne!

MARIANNE: *(to ELINOR)* Ewwww, I just heard that old guy say he loves me.

ELINOR: He is not old.

MARIANNE: He is at least 30. Which is ancient... old enough to be my father.

MRS. DASHWOOD: Excuse me, I'm 35. What do you think of me?

MARIANNE: Ummm... did not you hear him complain of the rheumatism?

ELINOR: When did he ever talk about rheumatism?

MARIANNE: Never mind. He totally loves me, and I am not into it.

MRS. DASHWOOD: *(to others)* We better get going. Thank you again for having us!

(ALL exit)

(ELINOR and MRS. DASHWOOD are talking; MARIANNE enters)

MARIANNE: Good Morning! Time to go for a walk! There is so much beauty in the morning light!

ELINOR: Calm down, Marianne.

MARIANNE: I can't calm down!! I have to tell everyone how much I appreciate nature!!

ELINOR: But it looks like it might rain.

MARIANNE: Even better! I'll appreciate the storm! What could possibly go wrong during a walk in the rain!

(MARIANNE exits)

ELINOR: She just jinxed that, didn't she?

MRS. DASHWOOD: Don't be so certain...

(WILLOUGHBY rushes on stage holding MARIANNE in his arms)

WILLOUGHBY: I am Willoughby! The rescuer of this fair lady!

ELINOR: I told you so.

MRS. DASHWOOD: *(gasps)* What happened??

WILLOUGHBY: She was dancing and singing in the rain and twisted her ankle. Thank goodness I was nearby, or she may have died!

(WILLOUGHBY sets MARIANNE down on the couch)

WILLOUGHBY: Marianne, I'm going to check on you every day and you will probably fall in love with me!

MARIANNE: I... I...

WILLOUGHBY: Shhh... don't speak, my dove. I'll see you tomorrow. *(runs offstage yelling)* She almost died! She almost died, and I saved her!

(enter SIR JOHN, COLONEL, and MRS. JENNINGS)

MRS. JENNINGS: Is Marianne okay? I heard she almost died!

ELINOR: It's only a sprained ankle, Mrs. Jennings. She's fine.

COLONEL: Marianne, can I get you anything?

ELINOR: She is fine. Everyone, go home now. I will take care of her.

(ALL exit except ELINOR, MARIANNE, and MRS. DASHWOOD)

ACT 1 SCENE 4

(ELINOR is drawing, MARIANNE reads, and MRS. DASHWOOD plays with a Rubik's Cube; SERVANT crosses with a sign that says, "The next day")

MARIANNE: Do you think it strange that Edward Ferrars has not come to visit us yet?

ELINOR: He is a busy man.

MRS. DASHWOOD: *(concentrating on cube)* I think he will visit us soon. It is of all things the most natural.

MARIANNE: I just think if he really liked Elinor, he would have come to visit already. At least sent a fruit basket or something.

(MARIANNE moves to the 'window')

ELINOR: Marianne, what are you doing?

MARIANNE: Huh? Nothing. Looking for your Edward and that fruit basket. I'm hungry.

(MARIANNE is staring longingly out the window)

ELINOR: Stop watching for Willoughby.

MARIANNE: What?! I wasn't!

(SERVANT enters)

SERVANT: Mr. Willoughby is here to call on Miss Marianne Dashwood.

(MARIANNE jumps up and squeals with excitement)

ELINOR: Marianne, show some propriety of self-command.

MARIANNE: Elinor, restraining my emotions is not merely an unnecessary effort, but a disgraceful subjection of reason to common-place and mistaken notions.

ELINOR: What?

MARIANNE: If I feel something, I'm going to show it! Love me or leave me, sister!

ELINOR: Oh, brother.

(WILLOUGHBY enters with a flourish and bows; MRS. DASHWOOD hides cube)

WILLOUGHBY: Dear Marianne! I see you are well!

MARIANNE: Yes, thank you. You saved my life!

WILLOUGHBY: It was nothing! And I have a present for you... a horse!

(WILLOUGHBY pulls a stick horse out from behind his back)

MARIANNE: Yay! A horse!! I will call him... Pecan!

ELINOR: Marianne, it is not in our mother's plan to keep any horse.

MARIANNE: Shush. He got me a horse and I want it. Besides, Pecan can hear you. We will ride every day!

WILLOUGHBY: Hurray! I have to go now. Bye!

(exit WILLOUGHBY)

ELINOR: Marianne, you can't accept that horse. He doesn't fit in the house and you barely know this Willoughby guy.

MARIANNE: You are mistaken, Elinor... I am much better acquainted with him, than I am with any other creature in the world, except yourself and mama.

ELINOR: Don't be ridiculous.

(MARIANNE pets the horse; enter SERVANT)

SERVANT: Mr. Edward Ferrars is here to call on Miss Dashwood.

MRS. DASHWOOD: I knew he would come visit!

(ELINOR fixes her hair and smooths her dress; enter EDWARD; SERVANT exits)

EDWARD: Good afternoon, ladies. I am pleased to see you after so long... Marianne, is that a horse?

MARIANNE: *(petting the horse)* Yep!

ELINOR: Hello, Mr. Ferrars. How nice of you to come and visit us!

EDWARD: Thank you for having me. You look beautiful... I MEAN... cool drawing.

ELINOR: You haven't even seen my drawing. But, thank you?

EDWARD: Oh yeah. Totally... I just knew it would be cool.

MRS. DASHWOOD: *(coughing)* How is Mrs. Ferrars, your mom? Has she convinced you to get a job yet?

EDWARD: I have no wish to be distinguished... Thank heaven! I cannot be forced into genius and eloquence.

MARIANNE: *(to herself)* No kidding.

(ELINOR glares at MARIANNE)

MRS. DASHWOOD: You have no ambition, I well know.

MARIANNE: *(muttering under her breath)* You mean he is boring and lazy.

EDWARD: Did you say something, Marianne?

(ELINOR tries to cover up Marianne's rudeness)

ELINOR: Marianne has not shyness to excuse any inattention of hers.

MARIANNE: I don't. What do you think of the village, Mr. Ferrars? Is not the landscape picturesque?

EDWARD: Yeah, it's cool.

MARIANNE: Cool? COOL?! Didn't you notice anything worth admiring?

EDWARD: You must not enquire too far, Marianne—remember I have no knowledge in the picturesque.

MARIANNE: You are so reserved!

EDWARD: Reserved! Am I reserved, Marianne?

MARIANNE: Yes, very.

EDWARD: How, in what manner? What am I to tell you?

MARIANNE: Ughhh! Anything! For Elinor's sake, I am happy you are here. But you have nothing exciting to say!

MRS. DASHWOOD: Marianne!

EDWARD: It's okay. I know Marianne is passionate about everything. I gotta go. Bye.

(EDWARD exits, moping as he goes)

ELINOR: I am going to draw upstairs.

(ELINOR sighs, exits opposite EDWARD)

MRS. DASHWOOD: *(to Marianne)* Now look at what you did.

MARIANNE: And you think it's a bad thing? He's soooo boring!

(ALL exit)

ACT 1 SCENE 5

(MARIANNE and WILLOUGHBY are whispering excitedly; ELINOR is chatting with MRS. DASHWOOD and MRS. JENNINGS; LADY MIDDLETON is sitting and looking bored)

SIR JOHN: *(to MRS. DASHWOOD)* I told you I host a lot of cool parties! Oh! I forgot the cookies!

(SIR JOHN exits)

MRS. JENNINGS: *(loud whispering to ELINOR)* I think Marianne and Mr. Willoughby are in love.

ELINOR: Mrs. Jennings! Have you heard Mr. Willoughby ever actually confess his feelings?

MRS. JENNINGS: No, but it is obvious.

(ELINOR looks alarmed; she glances over at MARIANNE and WILLOUGHBY; SERVANT enters with a letter on a tray and presents it to WILLOUGHBY who reads it)

WILLOUGHBY: *(standing)* I am now suffering under a very heavy disappointment!

MARIANNE: What's wrong?

WILLOUGHBY: I have to go on business to London.

MRS. DASHWOOD: To London!

MARIANNE: Noooooo!!

(MARIANNE runs offstage crying)

MRS. DASHWOOD: This is very unfortunate.

WILLOUGHBY: I will not torment myself any longer by hanging out with you guys. I will miss you all!

(WILLOUGHBY runs offstage crying)

ELINOR: It is all very strange! So suddenly to be gone!

MRS. DASHWOOD: Willoughby depends on his work. He will not confess to his engagement with Marianne, and will, instead, absent himself from Devonshire for a while.

MRS. JENNINGS: So, you think they are engaged too??

MRS. DASHWOOD: Oh, totally!

LADY MIDDLETON: Yes, totally obvious!

ELINOR: No! There has been total silence of both on the subject. Neither of them have spoken about an engagement!

(MARIANNE re-enters)

MARIANNE: My life is over! I'll probably never see Willoughby ever again! Ever, ever, EVER!

ELINOR: It's okay. Let's not be too dramatic.

MRS. DASHWOOD: Well, this is a melodrama, and it is Marianne.

MARIANNE: *(still crying)* Yeah. It's the perfect time to be dramatic.

MRS. JENNINGS: Wait! I have an idea! I am heading to London to help my pregnant daughter! Would you ladies like to accompany me?

ELINOR: I don't know...

MARIANNE: Yes! Yes! It would give me such happiness to be able to accept your invitation!

ELINOR: Mama, tell Marianne we cannot go. You need us here.

MRS. DASHWOOD: No, I don't. I am delighted with the plan.

MRS. JENNINGS: Good! Then it's settled!

(ALL exit; enter SIR JOHN holding tray of cookies, looking around)

SIR JOHN: What did I miss? *(exits)*

(MRS. JENNINGS, MARIANNE, and ELINOR enter)

ELINOR: You have a lovely London home, Mrs. Jennings.

MARIANNE: I need to write a letter to Willoughby!

(MARIANNE runs offstage; SERVANT enters)

SERVANT: There is a Colonel Brandon here.

(COLONEL enters)

MRS. JENNINGS: Oh! Colonel, I am monstrous glad to see you... But how did you know we were in town?

COLONEL: I had the pleasure of hearing it at your daughter's, where I have been dining.

MRS. JENNINGS: Oh! You did; How does my super pregnant daughter Charlotte do?

COLONEL: Mrs. Palmer appeared quite well... rounded.

(MARIANNE enters)

MARIANNE: I heard a man's voice! ... Oh. It's just you, Colonel.

COLONEL: Hello, Miss Marianne. It is lovely to see you again.

MRS. JENNINGS: Oh my! It looks like Colonel Brandon is as much in love with Marianne as ever!

(MARIANNE and COLONEL both look at MRS. JENNINGS with wide eyes; ELINOR smacks her hand against her forehead)

MARIANNE: *(to Elinor)* Has no letter been left here for me?

ELINOR: Marianne, we literally just arrived.

MARIANNE: So what?! Are you certain that no servant... has left any letter?

ELINOR: No.

MARIANNE: What about a carrier pigeon or an owl?

ELINOR: NO. Also... do you actually think mail travels by birds?

MARIANNE: Uhhh...

COLONEL: Anyway... I better get going. I will see all of you soon.

(COLONEL bows and exits)

ELINOR: Colonel Brandon is such a gentleman.

MARIANNE: He is old, and I don't care about him! Where is my sweet Willoughby?!

(MARIANNE runs offstage dramatically)

(enter ELINOR, MRS. PALMER, SIR JOHN, MARIANNE, MRS. JENNINGS, and any other party-goers that want to join onstage)

SIR JOHN: I cannot think of a better way to spend an evening than with nearly twenty young people, and to amuse them with a ball.

(everyone pairs off in groups and chat)

ELINOR: Mrs. Palmer! You haven't had your baby yet! Mrs. Jennings is very excited to be a grandma.

MRS. PALMER: Yeah, yeah... But let's get to the juicy gossip. I heard your sister is engaged to Mr. Willoughby.

ELINOR: Where did you hear that?

MRS. PALMER: From Colonel Brandon.

ELINOR: That doesn't seem like something Colonel Brandon would say.

MRS. PALMER: Well, he said it... with his eyes.

ELINOR: With his eyes?!

(enter COLONEL)

COLONEL: Elinor! I must speak with you!

ELINOR: What's wrong??

COLONEL: Your sister's engagement to Mr. Willoughby is very generally known.

MRS. PALMER: I told you so.

ELINOR: What is going on?! It cannot be generally known, for her own family do not know it.

(enter WILLOUGHBY escorting MISS GREY; MARIANNE runs up to ELINOR)

MARIANNE: Good heavens! He is there–he is there!

(ELINOR shakes MARIANNE by the shoulders)

ELINOR: Pray, pray be composed, and do not betray what you feel to everybody present.

MARIANNE: Go to him, Elinor, and force him to come to me.

(WILLOUGHBY walks over)

ELINOR: Too late. Here he comes.

(ALL step back and watch WILLOUGHBY and MARIANNE speak to each other)

WILLOUGHBY: Hello, Marianne.

MARIANNE: Hello, Willoughby.

WILLOUGHBY: I heard you were in town. I tried to call on you.

MARIANNE: I was hoping you would. There is something I have to tell you!

WILLOUGHBY: Me too!

(WILLOUGHBY and MARIANNE speak at the same time)

WILLOUGHBY: I'm engaged!

MARIANNE: I love you!

(ALL gasp)

MARIANNE: What? You're engaged? To me, right? Everyone keeps saying you are engaged to me.

WILLOUGHBY: Awkward... ummm... no. I am engaged to Miss Grey.

(MISS GREY waves from across the room)

MISS GREY: Hellooooo!

MARIANNE: *(to MISS GREY)* Don't wave at me! I don't know you!

WILLOUGHBY: My dear Madam... if I have been so unfortunate as to give rise to a belief of more than I felt, I am truly sorry.

MARIANNE: A rise to a belief? We are practically soul mates. You love me.

WILLOUGHBY: *(in a loud whisper to MARIANNE)* Okay, yes. I am in love with you. But I'm poor and have to marry Miss Grey for her money.

(MISS GREY waves again with a big smile)

WILLOUGHBY: I'm sorry, Marianne. Goodbye forever.

(WILLOUGHBY and MISS GREY exit; MARIANNE looks around)

ELINOR: Marianne, let me take you back...

MARIANNE: No, no, misery such as mine has no pride. I care not who knows that I am wretched.

(MARIANNE sobs melodramatically as she and ELINOR walk offstage; ALL exit)

(ELINOR sits alone, reading; enter SERVANT)

SERVANT: Colonel Brandon is here to see Miss Dashwood.

(COLONEL enters; SERVANT exits)

COLONEL: Miss Dashwood, there is something I must tell you. Mr. Willoughby is not a nice man! He proposed to my adopted daughter and then abandoned her!

ELINOR: Oh my! And you are afraid that this might happen to Marianne.

COLONEL: Precisely. His character is now before you.

ELINOR: Thank you for telling me.

COLONEL: Use your own discretion however, in communicating to Marianne what I have told you.

(COLONEL bows to ELINOR and exits; enter SERVANT)

SERVANT: There is a Miss Lucy Steele here to see Miss Dashwood.

ELINOR: Who?

(LUCY enters; SERVANT exits)

LUCY: Elinor, my very close friend, I must speak with you!

ELINOR: Do I know you?

LUCY: Yes of course! In an earlier part of the book, we established our friendship, but that scene was cut for time in this adaptation. See, right here. *(shows ELINOR pages in Sense & Sensibility book)*

ELINOR: Oh! That's right! *(to audience)* I actually find her quite annoying, but I am too nice to say anything.

LUCY: I can still hear you.

ELINOR: Oh, sorry. Go on.

LUCY: I simply must talk with you. I have a big, fat depressing secret... I am in love.

ELINOR: That's nice. With whom?

LUCY: Mr. Edward Ferrars! You know him, right?

ELINOR: You mean the man that I am also secretly in love with?

LUCY: What was that?

ELINOR: *(eyes wide)* Oh. Nothing. Uh... wow! So, you love Edward Ferrars!

LUCY: Yes! And not only am I in love... we have been engaged these four years.

ELINOR: Four years? Engaged?! I did not know that you were even acquainted.

LUCY: No one knows. And heaven knows how much longer we may have to wait to get married. Now you can feel miserable with me!

ELINOR: Great.

LUCY: Phew! I feel so much better now that you are sharing in my misery. I'll see you later!

(LUCY exits)

ELINOR: Why does everyone keep telling me their depressing secrets!

(ELINOR exits)

(enter MRS. JENNINGS, ELINOR, and MARIANNE)

MRS. JENNINGS: *(to audience)* This play is lasting quite long, we must wrap it up. *(to ELINOR)* Elinor! Lucy Steele and Edward Ferrars are secretly engaged!

ELINOR: How did you hear that?? Were you listening at the door?

MRS. JENNINGS: No! I heard it somewhere else. Apparently, Mr. Ferrars' family does not approve of their engagement and they disowned him.

(COLONEL enters)

COLONEL: Wait! I will be his patron, and he can work near my estate!

(EDWARD and LUCY enter)

EDWARD: Thank you so much, Colonel! Lucy, we will be poor, but now we have a place to live and we can get married!

LUCY: To me? No money? No thanks. I'll marry your brother instead since he will now inherit your family wealth. You can go be poor with what's-her-name.

(LUCY exits)

EDWARD: That stinks... but now I can marry my one true love! Elinor, will you marry me??

ELINOR: Yes!!

MARIANNE: Wait a minute. *(pulling ELINOR aside)* Elinor, don't you find it odd that he only chose you after Lucy rejected him?

ELINOR: Nope! He is a man of honor!

MARIANNE: Right...

ELINOR: Well, now I wish you had someone to marry, Marianne.

(COLONEL coughs to get their attention)

ELINOR: Wait! You can marry Colonel Brandon so that we can all live near each other!

MARIANNE: Sure, why not! I have matured a lot and realize that Willoughby wasn't right for me.

COLONEL: Score!

(MRS. DASHWOOD enters)

MRS. DASHWOOD: I seem to have missed something.

ELINOR: We are getting married!

MRS. DASHWOOD: Hurray! We won't die of poverty! What a wonderful ending! Oh, and I get grandkids, too! Let's go celebrate!

(ELINOR and MARIANNE look at each other with shocked eyes as MRS. DASHWOOD locks arms with girls and dances offstage)

THE END

Author's note and Special Thanks

S&S is my third Austen script. It is great fun to bring her works to life on the stage.

Special thanks go out to Mr. Rod's 2022-2023 6th Grade Theatre class at Pecan Trail Intermediate school. They did a beta class reading of S&S and gave some great advice! (hint: that's where the horse's name came from!) I always love the creative ideas the kids bring!

And as always, a big thank you to all our beta readers who are ALWAYS improving our scripts! Parisa, Isidro, Catherine, Royce, Katie, David E., Amanda, Lizette, David B., Kevin, Heather, Lisa, and Bridget. What a great list! Our books are not what their potential is, without our Betas!!!

Thanks as always!!!

-Brendan

Sneak Peeks at other
Playing With Plays books:

Tempest for Kids..Pg 84

Two Gentlemen of Verona for Kids.........................Pg 86

A Christmas Carol for Kids...............................Pg 89

Macbeth for Kids...Pg 94

The Oresteia for Kids....................................Pg 94

Beowulf for Kids...Pg 97

Jekyll & Hyde for Kids...................................Pg 99

The Tempest for Kids

PROSPERO: Hast thou, spirit, performed to point the tempest that I bade thee?

ARIEL: What? Was that English?

PROSPERO: *(Frustrated)* Did you make the storm hit the ship?

ARIEL: Why didn't you say that in the first place? Oh yeah! I rocked that ship! They didn't know what hit them.

PROSPERO: Why, that's my spirit! But are they, Ariel, safe?

ARIEL: Not a hair perished.

PROSPERO: Woo-hoo! All right. We've got more work to do.

ARIEL: Wait a minute. You're still going to free me, right, Master?

PROSPERO: Oh, I see. Is it sooooo terrible working for me? Huh? Remember when I saved you from that witch? Do you? Remember when that blue-eyed hag locked you up and left you for dead? Who saved you? Me, that's who!

ARIEL: I thank thee, master.

PROSPERO: I will free you in two days, okay? Sheesh. Patience is a virtue, or haven't you heard. Right. Where was I? Oh yeah... I need you to disguise yourself like a sea nymph and then... *(PROSPERO whispers something in ARIEL'S ear)* Got it?

ARIEL: Got it. *(ARIEL exits)*

PROSPERO: *(to MIRANDA)* Awake, dear heart, awake!

(MIRANDA yawns loudly)

PROSPERO: Shake it off. Come on. We'll visit Caliban, my slave.

MIRANDA: The witch's son? You mean the MONSTER! He's creepy and stinky!!!

PROSPERO: Mysterious and sneaky,

MIRANDA: Altogether freaky,

MIRANDA & PROSPERO: He's Caliban the slave!!! *(snap, snap!)*

PROSPERO: *(Calls offstage)* What, ho! Slave! Caliban!

(enter CALIBAN)

CALIBAN: Oh, look it's the island stealers! This is my home! My mother, the witch, left it to me and now you treat me like dirt.

MIRANDA: Oh boo-hoo! I used to feel sorry for you, I even taught you our language, but you tried to hurt me so now we have to lock you in that cave.

CALIBAN: I wish I had never learned your language!

PROSPERO: Go get us wood! If you don't, I'll rack thee with old cramps, and fill all thy bones with aches!

CALIBAN: *(to AUDIENCE)* He's so mean to me! But I have to do what he says. ANNOYING! *(exit CALIBAN)*

(enter FERDINAND led by "invisible" ARIEL)

ARIEL: *(Singing)* Who let the dogs out?! Woof, woof, woof!! *(Spookily)* The watchdogs bark; bow-wow, bow-wow!

FERDINAND: *(Dancing across stage)* Where should this music be? Where is it taking me! What's going on?

Sneak peek of

Two Gentlemen of Verona for Kids

ANTONIO: It's not nothing.

PROTEUS: Ahhhhh......It's a letter from Valentine, telling me what a great time he's having in Milan, yeah... that's what it says!

ANTONIO: Awesome! Glad to hear it! Because, you leave tomorrow to join Valentine in Milan.

PROTEUS: What!? Dad! No way! I don't want... I mean, I need some time. I've got some things to do.

ANTONIO: Like what?

PROTEUS: You know...things! Important things! And stuff! Lots of stuff!

ANTONIO: No more excuses! Go pack your bag. *(ANTONIO begins to exit)*

PROTEUS: Fie!

ANTONIO: What was that?

PROTEUS: Fiiii.......ne with me, Pops! *(ANTONIO exits)* I was afraid to show my father Julia's letter, lest he should take exceptions to my love; and my own lie of an excuse made it easier for him to send me away.

ANTONIO: *(Offstage)* Proteus! Get a move on!!

PROTEUS: Fie!!!

(exit)

ACT 2 SCENE 1

(enter VALENTINE and SPEED following)

VALENTINE: Ah, Silvia, Silvia! *(heavy sighs)*

SPEED: *(mocking)* Madam Silvia! Madam Silvia! Gag

me.

VALENTINE: Knock it off! You don't know her.

SPEED: Do too. She's the one that you can't stop staring at. Makes me wanna barf.

VALENTINE: I do not stare!

SPEED: You do. AND you keep singing that silly love song. *(sing INSERT SAPPY LOVE SONG)* You used to be so much fun.

VALENTINE: Huh? *(heavy sigh, starts humming SAME LOVE SONG)*

SPEED: Never mind.

VALENTINE: I have loved her ever since I saw her. Here she comes!

SPEED: Great. *(to audience)* Watch him turn into a fool.

(enter SILVIA)

VALENTINE: Hey, Silvia.

SILVIA: Hey, Valentine. What's goin' on?

VALENTINE: Nothin'. What's goin' on with you?

SILVIA: Nothin'.

(pause)

VALENTINE: What are you doing later?

SILVIA: Not sure. Prob-ly nothin'. You?

VALENTINE: Me neither. Nothin'.

SILVIA: Yea?

VALENTINE: Probably.

SPEED: *(to audience)* Kill me now.

SILVIA: Well, I guess I better go.

VALENTINE: Oh, okay! See ya'..

(pause)

SILVIA: See ya' later maybe?

VALENTINE: Oh, yea! Maybe! Yea! Okay!

SILVIA: Bye.

VALENTINE: Bye!

(exit SILVIA)

SPEED: *(aside)* Wow. *(to VALENTINE)* Dude, what the heck was that?

VALENTINE: I think she has a boyfriend. I can tell.

SPEED: Dude! She is so into you! How could you not see that?

VALENTINE: Do you think?

SPEED: Come on. We'll talk it through over dinner. *(to audience)* Fool. Am I right?

(exit)

Christmas Carol for Kids

(enter GHOST PRESENT wearing a robe and holding a turkey leg and a goblet)

GHOST PRESENT: Wake up, Scrooge! I am the Ghost of Christmas Present. Look upon me!

SCROOGE: I'm looking. Not that impressed. But let's get on with it.

GHOST PRESENT: Touch my robe! *(SCROOGE touches GHOST PRESENT's robe. Pause. They look at each other)* Er...it must be broken. Guess we walk. Come on. *(they begin walking downstage)*

SCROOGE: Where are we going?

GHOST PRESENT: Your employee, Bob Cratchit's house. Oh look, here we are.

(enter BOB, MRS. CRATCHIT, MARTHA CRATCHIT, and TINY TIM, who has a crutch in one hand; they are all holding bowls)

BOB: *(to audience)* Hi, we're the Cratchit family. We are a REALLY happy family!

MRS. CRATCHIT: *(to audience)* Yes, but we're REALLY poor, too. Thanks to HIS boss! *(pointing at BOB)*

MARTHA: *(to audience)* Yeah, as you can see our bowls are empty. *(shows empty bowl)* We practically survive off air.

TINY TIM: *(to audience)* But we're happy!

MRS. CRATCHIT: *(to audience; overly sappy)* Because we have each other.

TINY TIM: And love!

SCROOGE: *(to GHOST PRESENT)* Seriously, are they for real?

GHOST PRESENT: Yep! Adorable, isn't it?

BOB: A merry Christmas to us all.

TINY TIM: God bless us every one!

SCROOGE: Spirit, tell me if Tiny Tim will live.

GHOST PRESENT: *(puts hands to head as if looking into the future)* Ooooo, not so good....I see a vacant seat in the poor chimney corner, and a crutch without an owner. If SOMEBODY doesn't change SOMETHING, the child will die.

SCROOGE: No, no! Say he will be spared.

GHOST PRESENT: Nope, can't do that, sorry. Unless SOMEONE decides to change...hint, hint.

BOB: A Christmas toast to my boss, Mr. Scrooge! The founder of the feast!

MRS. CRATCHIT: *(angrily)* Oh sure, Mr. Scrooge! If he were here I'd give him a piece of my mind to feast upon. What an odious, stingy, hard, unfeeling man!

BOB: Dear, it's Christmas day. He's not THAT bad. *(Pause)* He's just... THAT sad. *(BOB holds up his bowl)* Come on, kids, to Scrooge! He probably needs it more than us!

MARTHA & TINY TIM: *(holding up their bowls)* To Scrooge!

MRS. CRATCHIT: *(muttering)* Thanks for nothing.

BOB: That's not nice.

MARTHA: And we Cratchits are ALWAYS nice. Read

the book, Mom.

MRS. CRATCHIT: Sorry.

(the CRATCHIT FAMILY exits)

SCROOGE: She called me odious! Do I really smell that bad?

GHOST PRESENT: Odious doesn't mean you stink. Although in this case you do... According to the dictionary, odious means "unequivocally detestable." I mean, you are a toad sometimes Mr. Scrooge.

SCROOGE: Wow... that's kind of ... mean.

Macbeth for Kids

ACT 2 SCENE 1

(DUNCAN runs on stage and dies with a dagger stuck in him, MACBETH drags his body off and then returns with the bloody dagger. LADY MACBETH enters)

LADY MACBETH: Did you do it?

MACBETH: *(clueless)* Do what?

LADY MACBETH: KILL HIM!

MACBETH: Oh yeah, all done. I have done the deed.

LADY MACBETH: *(pointing at the dagger)* What is that?

MACBETH: What?

LADY MACBETH: Why do you still have the bloody dagger with you?

MACBETH: Ummmmm, I don't know.

LADY MACBETH: Well go put it back!

MACBETH: NO! I'll go no more! I'm scared of the dark, and there is a dead body in there. I am afraid to think what I have done.

LADY MACBETH: Man you are a wimp, give me the dagger. *(LADY MACBETH takes the dagger, exits, and returns)*

LADY MACBETH: All done.

(there is a loud knock at the door)

LADY MACBETH: It's 2am! This really is not a good time for more visitors. *(goes to the door)* Who is it? *(opens door)*

　　　　

MACDUFF: It is Macduff. I am here to see the king.

MACBETH: He is sleeping in there.

(MACDUFF exits while MACBETH and LADY MACBETH look at each other)

MACDUFF: *(offstage scream)* AGHHHHHHHHHHH – He's dead, he's dead!!! *(MACDUFF enters)*

MACBETH: Who?

MACDUFF: Who do you think? *(they both scream)*

BANQUO: *(BANQUO, MALCOLM, and DONALBAIN enter)* What happened, can't someone get a good night sleep around here?

MACDUFF: The king has been murdered.

MALCOLM & DONALBAIN: Aghhhhhhhh!!!!!!!!!

DONALBAIN: We must be next.

MALCOLM: Let's get out of here.

DONALBAIN: I'm heading to Ireland.

MALCOLM: I'm off to England. *(MALCOLM and DONALBAIN exit)*

MACDUFF: Well, since there is no one left to be King, why don't you do it Mac?

LADY MACBETH & MACBETH: Okay. *(LADY MACBETH, MACBETH and MACDUFF exit)*

BANQUO: *(to audience)* I fear, thou play'dst most foully for't. *(MACBETH returns)*

MACBETH: Bank, what are you thinking over there?

BANQUO: Oh, nothing. *(said with a big fake smile)* Gotta go! See ya! *(BANQUO exits)*

The Oresteia for Kids

ACT 1 - Agamemnon

(Someone walks by with a sign that says, "PLAY 1 - AGAMEMNON"; CHORUS enters)

CHORUS 1: I hope we hear news of the war soon. Ten livelong years have rolled away since the Trojan War began.

CHORUS 2: Yes, the kingdom of Argos needs some good news for once.

CHORUS 3: *(to audience)* How did we get in this mess, you ask? Well, as elders, we know all the stories. Long ago, King Atreus was murdered by his brother.

(KING ATREUS enters and dies melodramatically)

CHORUS 1: Then his sons, Agamemnon and Menelaus, fled to Sparta.

(enter AGAMEMNON and MENELAUS)

MENELAUS: No, Dad!!!

KING ATREUS: My brother killed me! Avenge meeeee!!!! *(dies again)*

AGAMEMNON: We have to flee or we're next!

(AGAMEMNON and MENELAUS exit screaming)

CHORUS 2: But, the boys got lucky. The King of Sparta let Agamemnon marry his daughter, Clytemnestra.

(enter AGAMEMNON and CLYTEMNESTRA)

AGAMEMNON: I do!

CLYTEMNESTRA: I do, too!

(AGAMEMNON and CLYTEMNESTRA exit)

CHORUS: Awwwwe.

CHORUS 3: *(sniffling)* I always cry at weddings.

CHORUS 1: Then Menelaus became King of Sparta when their king died.

(enter MENELAUS wearing crown)

MENELAUS: I am the King of Sparta!

CHORUS 2: He also got to marry the king's other daughter, Helen, who is the most beautiful woman in the world.

(enter HELEN)

HELEN: I am. Let's go dear.

(MENELAUS and HELEN exit holding hands)

CHORUS 3: Agamemnon returned from Sparta, killed his uncle, and reclaimed the throne!

CHORUS 1: Oh, just like Hamlet!

CHORUS 2: No, like Lion King.

CHORUS 3: Would you two stop. Those stories were based on this story!

CHORUS 1&2: Cool!

CHORUS 3: So that's kind of how this current war got started. You see, a few years later, King Paris of Troy stopped in for a not-so-friendly visit.

(HELEN enters; PARIS enters opposite)

PARIS: You are the one Aphrodite promised me.

HELEN: I am?

PARIS: You shall come with me.

HELEN: I will?

(PARIS takes HELEN by the wrist and leads her offstage)

HELEN: HELP!!! Stranger danger!!!

CHORUS 1: They returned to Troy. Menelaus and his brother Agamemnon, Atreus' sons in vengeful ire, 'gainst Paris, started a war to get her back.

(enter AGAMEMNON and MENELAUS)

AGAMEMNON: Let's get your wife back!

AGAMEMNON & MENELAUS: Charge! *(both exit)*

CHORUS 2: But, a terrible price had to be paid at the start of this war. King Agamemnon made a fatal error.

CHORUS 3: He insulted the goddess Artemis, by boasting he was a better hunter than her. What hubris!

CHORUS 1: Bad idea. I've met Artemis. She's not just the goddess of the hunt, she's a friggin' furious warrior!

(enter ARTEMIS flanked by huntresses)

Sneak peek of
Beowulf for Kids
HROTHGAR and BEOWULF

(enter HROTHGAR and DANES)

HROTHGAR: *(wailing)* What have I done?! I have created a great hall and have put my people in danger! Hopefully, this monster will not come back again!

(exit HROTHGAR; enter GRENDEL)

GRENDEL: *(whistling; addresses audience)* Off to eat some more people! *(knocks at door, someone answers)* Rawwrr!!! I am the monster of evil, greedy and cruel, by the name of Grendel! Prepare to be eaten. . . again!

(GRENDEL eats some more people, wipes his mouth with a napkin, and runs off stage; enter HROTHGAR)

HROTHGAR: Noooooo! The monster has come back and will probably keep coming back for 12 years before someone comes to help us!

(HROTHGAR and his DANES wail loudly; DANE 2 crosses the stage with a sign that says "12 Years Later"; enter BEOWULF and GEAT SOLDIERS)

BEOWULF: I, the great and mighty Beowulf, warrior and champion of the Geats, servant to King Hygelac, have heard of your sorrows and have come to help!

(ALL stop crying)

HROTHGAR: How did you hear of our sorrows?

BEOWULF: *(leaning close to HROTHGAR, whispers)* Dude, you have been crying super loud for like 12 years, and I'm right offstage over there.

HROTHGAR: *(embarrassed, wipes face)* Oh right. *(cough)* Yes. Thank you for coming to our aid!

BEOWULF: I, the great Beowulf, alone now with Grendel I shall manage the matter, with the monster of evil.

HROTHGAR: Whew, that's a relief! I have been trying to figure out how to defeat Grendel for years and have failed. He's stopped by 4,380 times to feast on us!

BEOWULF: I never fail! I have defeated many a monster in my day! Including a sea monster. . . which is extra cool.

UNFERTH: Boooooo. That sea monster wasn't even that big!

BEOWULF: Who are you? And YES IT WAS!

UNFERTH: I am Unferth, great warrior for Hrothgar.

BEOWULF: *(to audience)* Obviously not THAT great. *(to UNFERTH)* You are just jealous of my greatness!

UNFERTH: Am not!

BEOWULF: Are too! And I heard you killed your brothers!

UNFERTH: Wow, that's a low blow... but... uhhhhh. . . . okay fine. I'll hang out right over here...

HROTHGAR: ANYWAY, back to me and MY problems.

BEOWULF: Right. Only with hand-grip the foe I must grapple, fight for my life then. If he win in the struggle, to eat in the war-hall earls of the geat-folk, boldly to swallow them.

GEAT SOLDIER 1: Wait. . . what was that?

BEOWULF: Sorry, quoting old text there. . . .I am going to fight Grendel with my bare hands. If I win, he dies. If I lose, he gets to eat all of us, including you!

Jekyll and Hyde
for Kids

UTTERSON: *(looks around)* Now, where is Hyde hiding?

NARRATOR: And they meet...

(enter HYDE)

UTTERSON: Mr. Hyde, I think?

HYDE: *(taken aback, and hisses)* That is my name. What's your issue?

UTTERSON: I am looking for Dr. Jekyll.

HYDE: He's not here.

UTTERSON: Let me see your face, sir.

HYDE: Why? Tell me how you know of me?

UTTERSON: We have common friends.

HYDE: *(snarls)* LIAR!!! *(suddenly exits)*

UTTERSON: Rude! *(to audience)* Did you see that murderous mixture of timidity and boldness? He seemed hardly human. I need to see Dr. Jekyll! *(walks across stage; knocks on door; POOLE enters)* Hello Poole, is Dr. Jekyll in?

POOLE: I'm sorry sir, but Dr. Jekyll is out.

UTTERSON: What can you tell me about Edward Hyde? I see he has a key to the back room.

POOLE: Ah, yes. Mr. Hyde has a key. We have orders to obey him.

UTTERSON: Thank you.

POOLE: Good day, sir. *(POOLE exits)*

UTTERSON: *(to audience)* That evil Hyde definitely has secrets of his own, black secrets. What has Jekyll gotten himself into?

(UTTERSON exits)

ACT 1 SCENE 3

Dr. Jekyll Was Quite at Ease

(enter DR. JEKYLL, UTTERSON)

NARRATOR: Soon, Dr. Jekyll hosted a party, and Utterson was determined to question his dear old friend...

JEKYLL: Thank you for coming to my pleasant dinner party. I always enjoy your company, Mr. Utterson.

UTTERSON: I've been wanting to speak to you, Jekyll. You know that will of yours?

JEKYLL: You are unfortunate in such a client. I never saw a man so distressed as you were by my will.

UTTERSON: You know I never approved of it.

JEKYLL: Yes, you have told me so.

UTTERSON: Well, I tell you again. Because I have learned more of young Hyde. What I heard was abominable.

JEKYLL: *(surprised)* Listen to me. DROP THIS. You do not understand my position.

UTTERSON: Jekyll, I am a man to be trusted. I am a lawyer. *(NARRATOR starts laughing; to NARRATOR)* Don't laugh.

NARRATOR: Sorry, you said "trust" and "lawyer" in the same sentence. And...yeah... My bad. Go on.

UTTERSON: *(to JEKYLL)* Tell me in confidence and I can get you out of it.

JEKYLL: I can be rid of Mr. Hyde when I choose. This is a private matter, and I beg of you to let it sleep.

UTTERSON: Fine, I will let it go... for now.

JEKYLL: Good.

ABOUT THE AUTHORS

AMANDA THAYER loves books more than most things *(excepting maybe her husband and children)*. She has a B.A. in English and a Master of Library Studies from the University of North Carolina at Greensboro. She is also an actress and dramaturg, having worked with SLO Repertory Theatre, The Great American Melodrama, and PCPA. Amanda grew up performing and understands the importance of youth arts programs. Amanda likes to laugh and she hopes you do too!

BRENDAN P. KELSO came to writing modified Shakespeare scripts when he was taking time off from work to be at home with his newly born son. "It just grew from there". Within months, he was being asked to offer classes in various locations and acting organizations along the Central Coast of California. Originally employed as an engineer, Brendan never thought about writing. However, his unique personality, humor, and love for engaging the kids with The Bard has led him to leave the engineering world and pursue writing as a new adventure in life! He has always believed, "the best way to learn is to have fun!" Brendan makes his home on the Central Coast of California and loves to spend time with his wife and kids.

CAST AUTOGRAPHS

www.ingramcontent.com/pod-product-compliance
Lightning Source LLC
Chambersburg PA
CBHW061028050726
47592CB00004B/1383